MORE CRAZY LAWS

by Dick Hyman

(author of CRAZY LAWS)

Illustrated by Don Orehek

SCHOLASTIC INC.
New York Toronto London Auckland Sydney

ISBN 0-590-45389-0

12 11 10 9 8 7 6 5 4 3 2 1   2 3 4 5 6 7/9

Printed in the U.S.A.   01

First Scholastic printing, January 1992

INTRODUCTION

Did you know that it's against the law:

• to raise chickens in bottles in New Jersey?
• for monkeys to ride on buses in San Antonio, Texas?
• to paint a horse in Vermont?

Ridiculous? Incredible? Unbelievable? No! These and loads of other loony laws are real. Many of these laws go back to the horse-and-buggy days. Although a few have been canceled by now, many still remain on the books. Prepare to be amazed and get ready for lots of laughs as you read this collection of the silliest laws you've every heard of!

LAYING DOWN THE LAW

Donkeys are not allowed to sleep in bathtubs in Brooklyn, New York.

It is illegal to fall asleep under a hair drier in Florida.

In San Jose, California, it is illegal to sleep in your neighbors' outhouse without their permission.

It's against the law in North Dakota to go to bed wearing shoes.

In Anniston, Alabama, it is illegal for any person to sleep in the city streets at any time.

A hobo must consult the president of a railroad company before he can take a nap in an empty boxcar without breaking the law in Wichita, Kansas.

It is illegal in Pittsburgh, Pennsylvania, to sleep in a refrigerator.

In Ola, South Dakota, an ordinance prohibits a person from taking a rest in the middle of the road.

In Detroit, Michigan, it is against the law to fall asleep in the bathtub.

A Kentucky law says that it is illegal to sleep in a restaurant.

DISTURBING THE PEACE

It's against the law for cats to howl after 9 P.M. in Columbus, Georgia.

A Barker, New Jersey, law makes it illegal to knock on doors or ring doorbells.

A Dunn, North Carolina, law prohibits snoring that disturbs the neighbors.

In North Little Rock, Arkansas, a city law says that a person may not scream, shout, or sing on the street.

Loud or boisterous talking at a picnic is prohibited in Pennsylvania.

A St. Louis, Missouri, law makes it illegal to talk in church.

A Wichita, Kansas, law prohibits the playing of electric pianos and banjos between 11:30 P.M. and 9 A.M.

A Louisiana law states that it is illegal to whistle on Sunday.

In New Jersey, a person can be arrested for slurping soup.

DISORDERLY CONDUCT

A law in Wichita, Kansas, makes it illegal to throw confetti.

In Chillicothe, Missouri, it is against the law to throw rice at weddings.

In Klamath Falls, Oregon, it is against the law to kick the heads of snakes.

A 1929 Nebraska law made it illegal to "disturb" honeybees.

In Los Angeles it is against the law to complain through the mails that a hotel has cockroaches, even if it is true.

In Zion City, Illinois, it is illegal to make ugly faces at anyone.

It is against the law in Salt Lake City, Utah, to carry a ukelele on the street if it isn't wrapped up.

It is against the law to carry an open umbrella down the sidewalk on Central Avenue in Hot Springs, Arkansas.

A Shreveport, Louisiana, law will fine anyone who carries a concealed crochet needle, ruling it a dangerous weapon.

It is illegal to hypnotize anyone in Moscow, Idaho.

Boys are forbidden to throw snowballs at trees within the city limits of Mt. Pulaski, Illinois.

In Corning, Iowa, it is against the law to speak to anyone passing along the street or sidewalk.

A Georgia law says that anyone who eavesdrops — or tries to eavesdrop — is a criminal and is subject to punishment for a misdemeanor.

IT'S CRIMINAL!

In 1924 a monkey was convicted in South Bend, Indiana, of the crime of smoking a cigarette, and was sentenced to pay a fine of $25 and the cost of the trial.

A Kentucky law says that burglary can only be committed at night.

In Illinois an animal may be sent to jail.

In Natchez, Mississippi, it is illegal for elephants to drink beer.

In Topeka, Kansas, it is illegal for a waiter to serve wine in a teacup.

It is unlawful for a man or woman to go unshaven in Carizozo, New Mexico.

It is unlawful to keep a prisoner in jail on Sundays in Kulmont, Pennsylvania.

A White Cloud, Kansas, law makes it illegal to break out of jail.

In Idaho fishing from the back of any animal is illegal.

In Houston, Mississippi, it's illegal to get on or off a train without a health certificate.

In Hanover, California, it's illegal to prevent children from jumping over puddles.

DOGGONE IT —
IT'S THE LAW!

Dogs are forbidden to bark between 8 P.M. and 6 A.M. in Collingwood, New Jersey.

In Little Rock, Arkansas, it's against the law for dogs to bark after 6 P.M.

A Wanamassa, New Jersey, law prohibits dogs from crying.

In Boston, Massachusetts, it is illegal to keep a dog more than ten inches in height.

It is illegal to tie a tin box to a dog in Calhoun, Georgia.

In Paulding, Ohio, a police officer may bite a barking dog to quiet him.

In Sheridan, Wyoming, it is unlawful to permit any dog to stand closer than ten feet to a fire hydrant within city limits.

THESE LAWS ARE FOR THE BIRDS

In Massachusetts it's against the law to allow a chicken in a bakery.

Roosters are forbidden to crow within the city limits of Ontario, California.

Essex Fells, New Jersey, forbids dogs to bark, roosters to crow, and ducks to quack between the hours of 10 P.M. and 6 A.M.

Pigeons are not permitted to fly over Bellevue, Kentucky.

A Berkeley, California, law forbids anyone to whistle for a lost canary before 7 A.M.

An old Truro, Massachusetts, law says that a man can't get married until he has killed six blackbirds or three crows.

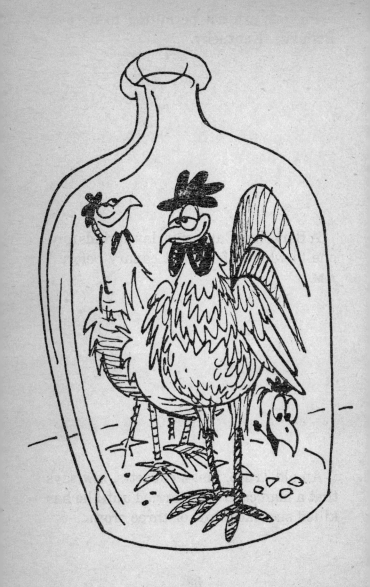

It's unlawful to raise chickens in bottles in New Jersey.

LAWS THAT DON'T MAKE HORSE SENSE

In Vermont it's a crime to paint a horse.

In Washington, D.C., it is illegal to cut off the tail of any horse.

It is against the law to tie horses to fire hydrants in St. Louis, Missouri.

Horse racing is illegal on the streets of El Paso, Texas.

In Lourdsburg, New Mexico, it is against the law for mules to visit a saloon.

A bill passed by the Arkansas legislature prohibits mule owners from filing their animals' teeth.

An Iowa state law forbids any person to keep a horse in the rooms of an apartment house.

A California law prohibits a person from entering a tavern on horseback.

In Boston a hotel owner must put up and bed down the horse of a guest.

MORE LOONY ANIMAL LAWS

In Minneapolis, Minnesota, it is unlawful to tease or torment skunks.

It is perfectly legal for sheep to graze on Baldwin Hill in Los Angeles just so long as they nibble more than two inches from the ground.

No lions shall be allowed to run wild on the streets of Alderson, West Virginia.

It is unlawful to hitch a crocodile to a fire hydrant in Michigan.

In Manville, New Jersey, it is illegal to feed animals whiskey or cigarettes in a public park.

It's against the law for mongooses to enter the United States.

A U.S. postal law prohibits sending mice through the mail.

56

In Knoxville, Tennessee, it's against the law to lasso a fish.

A San Antonio, Texas, law forbids monkeys to ride on buses.

It is illegal for a cow to cross a road after sundown in Missouri.

It is illegal to wash animals on city streets in Knoxville, Tennessee.

A Kentucky law prohibits bullfighting.

It's against the law to feed your hogs on the sidewalks in Gainsville, Alabama.

A Nottingham, Maryland, law says that hogs must be allowed to roam loose between March 1 and October 20.

FASHION POLICE?

A Saco, Missouri, law forbids any person to wear a hat that might frighten children or animals.

In Yonkers, New York, it's against the law to tie your shoes when you're in the middle of the sidewalk.

In Maine it is against the law to walk through the streets with shoelaces undone.

In Portsmouth, Ohio, no one may drive a car without wearing shoes.

Guests at weddings who throw shoes are breaking the law in Colorado.

It's against the law for employees to work barefooted in Concord, New Hampshire.

In Pine Island District, Minnesota, it is illegal for a man to pass a cow without tipping his hat.

It is illegal for a woman to wear a bracelet watch on her ankle in Elizabethton, Tennessee.

In Nogales, Arizona, a law prohibits wearing suspenders.

It is illegal for a man to appear on the streets of Dallas Center, Iowa, without a shirt.

THESE LAWS ARE ALL WET!

In Durango, Colorado, no one may swim in the daytime in any pool or river within the city limits.

An old Georgia law says that every lifeguard must wear a solid bright red bathing suit with a leather harness around his or her neck attached to a lifeline 200 feet long.

In Carmel, California, it is illegal for a lady to take a bath in a business office.

An Indiana law makes it illegal to take a bath in the wintertime.

It's against the law in Portland, Oregon, to bathe without wearing a bathing suit covering you from your neck to your knees.

In Georgia, on Sunday, anyone bathing in a stream or pond in the view of a road leading to a church is guilty of a misdemeanor.

In Prichard, Alabama, a law says that every man must wear a top to his bathing suit.

In the winter months in Tucson, Arizona, it is illegal to show oneself in public dressed in a bathing suit.

DAFFY TRAFFIC LAWS

In Moscow, Idaho, it is illegal to ride a tricycle on the sidewalk.

In Logansport, Indiana, it's against the law to wheel a baby carriage on the sidewalk.

An Oregon traffic law says: "The car that beats the other cars to an intersection has the right of way."

An old Connecticut law forbids anyone to ride a bicycle more than 65 miles an hour.

The Georgia supreme court ruled that it is not necessary for a train engineer to blow his whistle for each individual cow on the tracks.

In Gainesville, Florida, no train may run through the city faster than a man can walk.

An old Arkansas law states that an automobile must be preceded by a man carrying a red flag.

In New Orleans a fire engine must stop for red traffic lights when going to a fire.

In Santa Ana, California, it is illegal to pass a fire truck while riding a bicycle.

PLAYING BY THE RULES

An Arkansas law makes it unlawful to play cards on Sunday.

An old law in La Crosse, Wisconsin, prohibits playing checkers in public.

According to Baltimore, Maryland, city code, every man, woman, or child who has bowled a game since 1833 is subject to a fine of two dollars for each offense.

In Alabama it is illegal to play dominoes on Sunday.

In Alabama it is unlawful to play bridge at any hotel.

ALL KINDS OF LOONY LAWS

You have a legal right to grow as tall as you like in Los Angeles.

An attorney general in Connecticut ruled that if you are a beaver you have a right to build dams.

In Oregon a dead juror cannot serve on a jury.

In Detroit, Michigan, it's against the law to sit in the middle of the street and read the newspaper.

It is against the law in Alabama for anyone to buy a bag of peanuts after sunset and before sunrise of the next day.

Section 8726 of Burns, Indiana, Statutes of 1926 says that bed sheets in hotels must be at least 99 inches long and 81 inches wide.

The state of Arkansas forbids a waiter to receive a tip from a guest.

The Wisconsin legislature passed a bill making it compulsory for all boarding-houses, clubs, hotels, and restaurants to serve at least two thirds of an ounce of cheese with every meal sold at 25 cents or more.

A San Francisco law prohibits carrying, on sidewalks, bags or baskets suspended from poles.

The United States Supreme Court ruled in 1893 that the tomato was a vegetable and not a fruit.

A St. Louis, Missouri, law makes it illegal to erect a barbed-wire fence within the city limits.